T H E
FRIENDLY BEASTS

THE FRIENDLY BEASTS

A TRADITIONAL CHRISTMAS CAROL

ILLUSTRATED BY SARAH CHAMBERLAIN

DUTTON CHILDREN'S BOOKS   NEW YORK

"THE FRIENDLY BEASTS"
is a medieval Christmas carol that dates from the twelfth century.

Illustrations copyright © 1991
by Sarah Chamberlain

All rights reserved.

Published in the United States by
Dutton Children's Books,
a division of Penguin Books USA Inc.

Designer: Joseph Rutt

Printed in Hong Kong
by South China Printing Co.

First Edition

Library of Congress Cataloging-in-Publication Data

The Friendly beasts / illustrated by Sarah Chamberlain.
   p. cm.
  Summary: In this old English Christmas carol, the friendly
stable beasts tell of the gifts they have given to the
newborn Jesus.
  ISBN 0-525-44773-3
  1. Carols, English—Texts. 2. Christmas music. 3. Folk-songs,
English—Texts. [1. Carols—England. 2. Christmas music.
3. Folk songs—England.] I. Chamberlain, Sarah, ill.
PZ8.3.F91188 1991
782.28'1723—dc20   91-2115 CIP AC

The illustrations are multicolor linoleum block prints
that have been highlighted by hand with pastels.

10 9 8 7 6 5 4 3 2 1

For Jamie and Jim

Jesus, our brother, kind and good
Was humbly born in a stable rude.
And the friendly beasts around Him stood,
Jesus, our brother, kind and good.

"I," said the donkey, shaggy and brown,
"I carried His mother uphill and down,
 I carried her safely to Bethlehem town."
"I," said the donkey, shaggy and brown.

"I," said the cow, all white and red,
"I gave Him my manger for His bed,
  I gave Him my hay to pillow His head."
"I," said the cow, all white and red.

"I," said the dove from the rafters high,
"Cooed Him to sleep, that He should not cry,
We cooed Him to sleep, my mate and I."
"I," said the dove from the rafters high.

"I," said the rooster, with the shining eye,
"I crowed the news up to the sky.
 When the sun arose, I crowed to the sky."
"I," said the rooster, with the shining eye.

"I," said the sheep with the curly horn,
"I gave Him my wool, for His blanket warm.
 He wore my coat on Christmas morn."
"I," said the sheep with the curly horn.

"I," said the camel, all yellow and black,
"Over the desert upon my back,
    I brought Him a gift in a wise man's pack."
"I," said the camel, all yellow and black.

So every beast by some good spell,
In the stable dark was glad to tell
Of the gift he gave Emmanuel.
The gift he gave Emmanuel.

THE FRIENDLY BEASTS

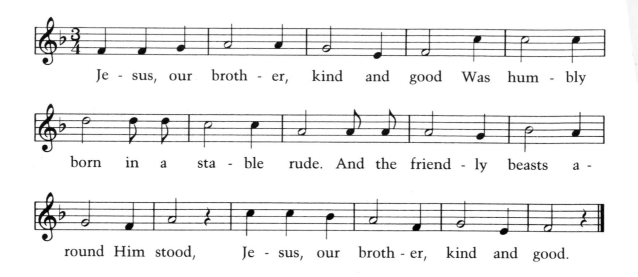

Je - sus, our broth - er, kind and good Was hum - bly
born in a sta - ble rude. And the friend - ly beasts a -
round Him stood, Je - sus, our broth - er, kind and good.

"I," said the donkey, shaggy and brown,
"I carried His mother uphill and down,
 I carried her safely to Bethlehem town."
"I," said the donkey, shaggy and brown.

"I," said the cow, all white and red,
"I gave Him my manger for His bed,
 I gave Him my hay to pillow His head."
"I," said the cow, all white and red.

"I," said the dove from the rafters high,
"Cooed Him to sleep, that He should not cry,
 We cooed Him to sleep, my mate and I."
"I," said the dove from the rafters high.

"I," said the rooster, with the shining eye,
"I crowed the news up to the sky.
 When the sun arose, I crowed to the sky."
"I," said the rooster, with the shining eye.

"I," said the sheep with the curly horn,
"I gave Him my wool, for His blanket warm.
 He wore my coat on Christmas morn."
"I," said the sheep with the curly horn.

"I," said the camel, all yellow and black,
"Over the desert upon my back,
 I brought Him a gift in a wise man's pack."
"I," said the camel, all yellow and black.

So every beast by some good spell,
In the stable dark was glad to tell
Of the gift he gave Emmanuel.
The gift he gave Emmanuel.